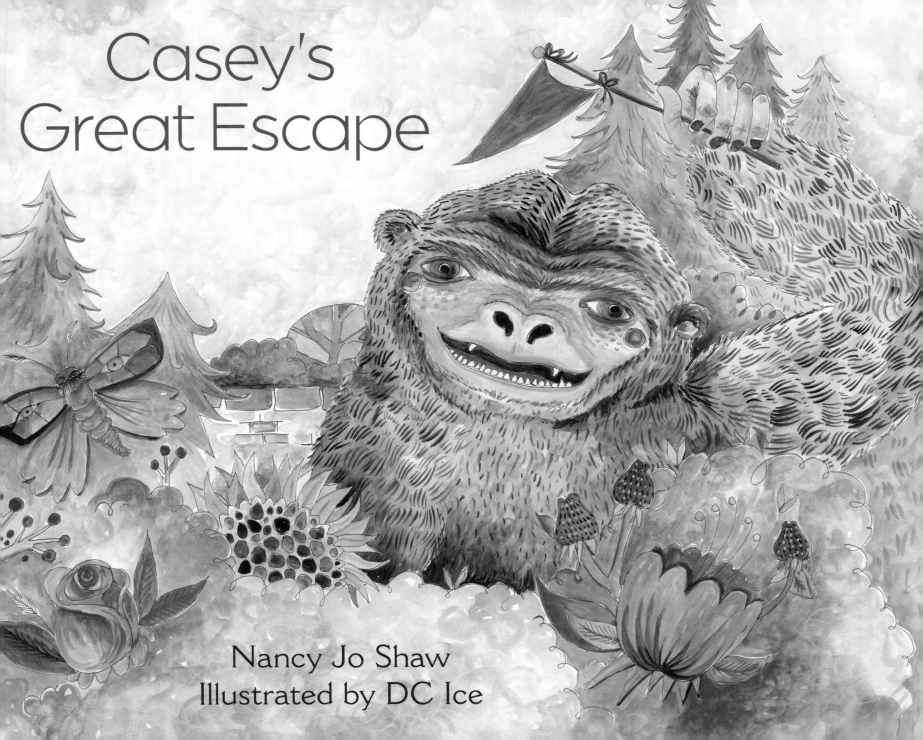

Casey's Great Escape

Nancy Jo Shaw

Illustrated by DC Ice

Award-winning author NANCY JO SHAW of Mendota Heights, Minnesota delights us with yet another whimsical tale—this time about a gorilla named Casey. Raising her family and teaching school in the Como Park neighborhood of St. Paul, Minnesota, she frequently visited the zoo with her three sons and students from Chelsea Heights Elementary. Now a retired teacher and proud grandmother, she still enjoys visiting Como Park Zoo and Conservatory where she and her husband are members of Como Friends. "I've been working on this gorilla story ever since the day Casey escaped way back in 1994," she says, "and now twenty years later I've finished it." Among Nancy's published works are six other children's books, including *Give Her a Pixie* and *Spring Is Here*. Visit her at www.nancy-jo-shaw.com.

Since graduating from The College of Visual Arts, DC ICE has illustrated over a dozen children's books. She is passionate about unfolding stories through artwork. *Casey's Great Escape* wonderfully depicts her love of exploring human-like emotions in animals. In addition to her illustrations, DC creates critter-filled paintings. Although she exhibits extensively in the Twin Cities area, her paintings are also shown nationally. DC lives and works in a historic artist loft in St. Paul, Minnesota with her creative husband, Matthew. See her paintings and find out about upcoming art exhibits at www.dcice.com.

ISBN 13: 978-1-59298-774-0

Library of Congress Control Number: 2016915068

Printed in the United States of America

First Printing: 2017

20 19 18 17 16   5 4 3 2 1

Cover and interior design by Laura Drew.
Edited by Laurie Flanigan Hegge.

Beaver's Pond Press
7108 Ohms Lane
Edina, MN 55439-2129
952-829-8818
www.beaverspondpress.com

To my three amazing sons,
Hans, Peter, and Nathan Grinager,
and to all the wonderful family time spent
in Como Park Zoo and Conservatory.

Casey Gorilla knew just what he'd do
When he woke up one morning in our City Zoo.
For weeks he'd been planning his *great escape*,
Flexing his muscles to get into shape.

Casey had fun in his outdoor play spaces
But wanted to visit exciting new places.
He knew other animals lived nearby,
He could hear them at night,
    when they'd chatter and cry.

The lions roared loudly, striped tigers did too,
Even white polar bears growled at the zoo.
From the space where he lived, Casey heard every sound,
And he longed to get out and wander around.
He wanted to meet all the other zoo creatures
And see their unique and interesting features.

Casey wondered . . .
How far does a giraffe's neck stretch in the air?
How many stripes does a zebra wear?

What does a lion's mane really look like?
Can Sparky the sea lion pedal a bike?

Casey, the curious African gorilla,
Was tired of acting so very *vanilla.*
He was a brave, hairy silverback beast.
Nothing could frighten him, not in the least!

Zookeeper Zoey was always impressed
When she saw Casey pounding his chest.
But she didn't hear what his friends heard him say:

"HEY, EVERYBODY, TODAY IS THE DAY!"

Then Casey Gorilla stood at the edge
Of his concrete wall with his feet on the ledge,
Ready to jump in a ditch, deep and wide
And scale up a wall on the far other side.
Oodles of people were there at the zoo,
But Casey was certain of what he must do.

His gorilla friends cheered...

"GO, CASEY, GO!
YOU'RE A ROCK STAR!
GIVE IT A TRY!
IT ISN'T THAT FAR!"

So Casey lept down, climbed up, and soon landed
Over the fence—he was no longer stranded!
"I made it! I did it! I'm out! I am free!
Who will I meet now, and what will I see?"

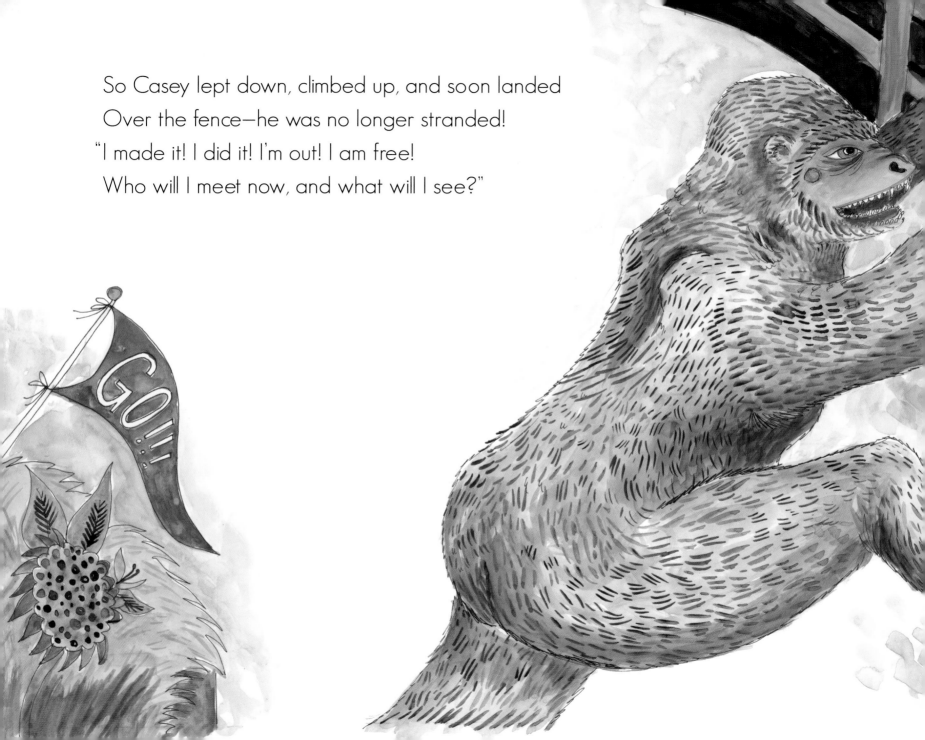

But Casey Gorilla did not journey far
Before he stepped into some freshly laid tar.
His large hairy feet felt all gooey and sticky.
NOW his adventure was icky and tricky.

It didn't take long before he heard a shout.
The whole zoo was abuzz,

"THE GORILLA
IS OUT!"

Before Casey knew which way he should run,
The zookeeper came with a tranquilizer gun.
She took her aim straight at Casey's behind...

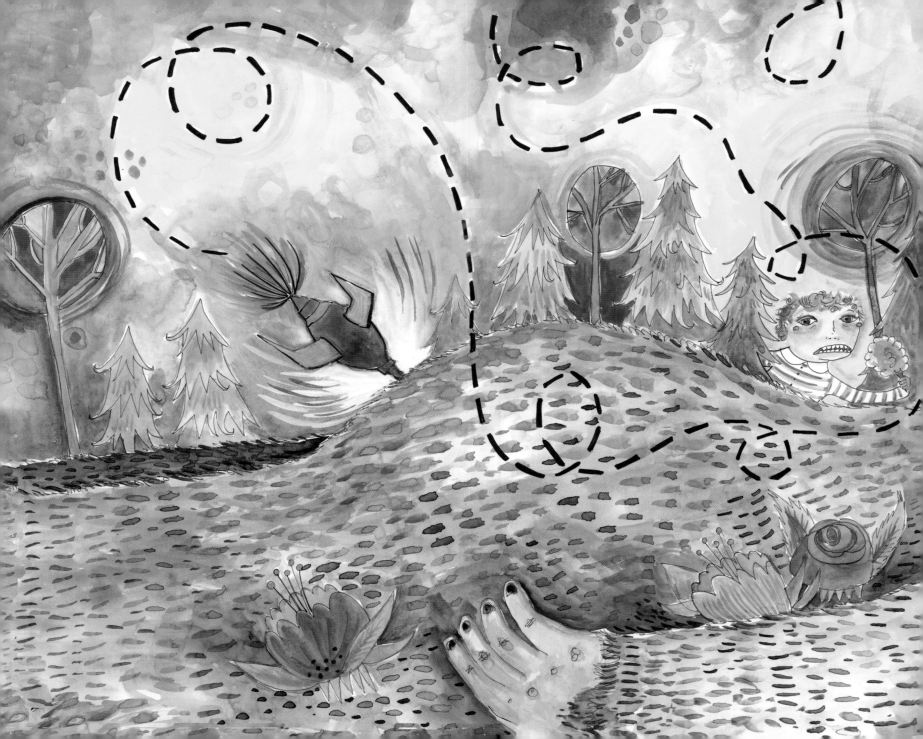

And he soon fell asleep with strange thoughts in his mind.
(He dreamt he saw bison in rich fields of clover.)
Time to go home. His adventure was over.

Once he was back with the rest of his band
He pondered how things hadn't gone as he'd planned.
"I know I have other friends here at the zoo,
But what are they like? I sure wish I knew.

Now I will never know how my friends look,
Unless I see pictures of them in a book."

Zookeeper Zoey knew Casey's great wish,
And gave him a book about critters and fish.
This book kept Casey quite happy and busy,
But now ALL the zookeepers were in a tizzy!

They needed to fix the gorillas' play space,
So all the great apes would stay in one place.
They built a strong fence on top of the wall,
Making the wall too tall to crawl.

Soon the report of Casey's big caper
Made the front page
    of our city newspaper.

CASEY the GORILLA'S GREAT ESCAPE

Can you guess why I know this is true?
Because I was there on that day at the zoo!

Just imagine
    if you'd been there too!

Notes from the Author

We WERE at our city zoo, the **Como Park Zoo of St. Paul, Minnesota** on May 13, 1994, but had gone home just before a 400-pound silverback western lowland gorilla named Casey climbed out of his outdoor play space. I have often wondered why Casey wanted to get out that day. Whatever his reason, this rhyming story is my rhythmic rendition of the event, meant only to entertain my readers by stretching the truth and personifying the gorilla.

Casey's real-life adventure lasted forty-five minutes before he saw a zookeeper holding a tranquilizer gun and was escorted back to his designated space. (He was not actually shot with a dart as he was in my story.) No one was hurt, and the zoo placed a wooden barrier around the gorilla enclosure to keep it from happening again.

Shortly after this escapade, Casey was moved from the Como Park Zoo to the Audubon Zoo in New Orleans, Louisiana where he is still a crowd favorite, interacting with human zoo visitors, especially babies and children.

When Casey made his escape, he left his big footprints in a newly tarred asphalt sidewalk outside his gorilla enclosure. Afterwards, the Como Zoo staff painted gorilla footprints on the path retracing Casey's actual steps. For years, my three sons enjoyed walking on Casey's tracks, until over time the paint faded away.

In June 2013, Como Park Zoo opened a new exhibit called **Gorilla Forest.** This spacious outdoor habitat is entirely enclosed, making it safe and secure for the gorillas as they interact within their troop. Zoo visitors observe their unique primate behaviors and physical traits while learning about gorilla preservation. Como Park Zoo educates the public about critical gorilla issues and ways humans can help gorillas by offering excellent information, classes, and programs for school children and groups.

Como Park Zoo participates in the **Gorilla Species Survival Plan (SSP)** along with the fifty other North American zoos that house gorillas. Currently there are a total of 353 western lowland gorillas housed within these accredited zoos. The fact that gorillas are a **critically endangered species** is exactly why zoos like Como are crucial to the survival of the worldwide gorilla population through the maintenance of healthy, genetically diverse, and self-sustaining gorillas.

The average lifespan of gorillas is thirty-five to forty-five years in the wild, and up to fifty years or more within captivity. Casey celebrated his thirty-fourth birthday on June 28, 2016 at the Audubon Zoo, where he still resides. Thanks for inspiring this story, Casey. Long may you reign!